In the Sky
ACTIVITY BOOK

by Devra Newberger Speregen
Illustrations by Christine Finn

SCHOLASTIC INC.
New York   Toronto   London   Auckland   Sydney

No part of this publication may be reproduced in whole or in part, or stored in a retrieval system, or transmitted in any form or by any means, electronic, mechanical, photocopying, recording, or otherwise, without written permission of the publisher. For information regarding permission, write to Scholastic Inc., 730 Broadway, New York, NY 10003.

ISBN 0-590-47591-6

12 11 10 9 8 7 6 5 4 3 2 1   3 4 5 6 7 8/9

Printed in the U.S.A.   34

First Scholastic printing, September 1993

You can check your answers to puzzles in this book on pages 31 and 32.

Sun-sational!

Compared to Earth, the sun is *huge*! In fact, if the sun were hollow, it could hold 1.3 million Earths inside! The sun is about 93 million miles away from Earth, but its rays are strong enough to give our planet light and help organisms grow.

How many times can you find the word SUN in the puzzle? You can look up, down, backward, and forward. Circle each word as you find it.

```
S S U N
N U S U
U N U S
S U N U
```

What Is It?

Believe it or not, the sun is not a planet — it is a *star*. And a medium-sized one at that. The sun appears bigger and brighter than other stars in the sky because it is much closer to us than those stars. Ninety-three million miles might not *sound* close, but the next closest star to Earth is about 25 *million million* miles away!

Draw a line to match each star with one that's exactly the same size.

Moon Struck!

The moon has no light of its own! Then how does it shine?
The moon shines because it catches some light from the faraway sun!
The sun's light is so strong, it lights up the moon.

Some nights — when there is a full moon — the sun lights up the moon
so strongly that we can see outside almost as if it were daytime.

**Look at this moonlit scene. There are five owls in it.
Owls are birds that stay awake at night. Circle these
nighttime creatures as you find them.**

Now That's Hot!

Everyone knows the sun is hot. But just how hot is it? Since spaceships could never get close enough to the sun to find out, scientists can only guess at how hot it is. They say that the temperature at the sun's core could reach as high as 27 million degrees! *Whew!*

Summertime is when the earth is tilted toward the sun. Since the sun is so hot, temperatures in the summer can go as high as 100 degrees!

Color this summertime scene any way you like.

Clouds, Clouds Everywhere!

Some days there are no clouds in the sky. On other days all you can see are big, puffy white clouds. They may *look* like enormous cotton balls, but clouds are actually masses of moisture in the air.

People say that no two clouds are alike, but there *are* two clouds that are the same in this picture. Can you find them?

Up and Away!

There are many things we see when we look up into the sky. On a clear day, we can see the sun, an airplane, birds, a hot-air balloon, clouds, and sometimes even a faint moon!

Find the words SUN, AIRPLANE, BIRDS, BALLOON, CLOUDS, and MOON in this word search. You can look forward, backward, up, and down. Circle each word as you find it.

M O O N B D E B
N U S O A R A L
C B D S L M G R
A I R P L A N E
H R C L O U D S
I D S K O F O N
T S J H N E P Q

11

A-Mazing Moon Journey!

If you could visit the moon — and someday you might — you would see that it is covered with dust. There is no water. There is no air. There is little *gravity* to keep things from floating away. In the sunshine, it is hotter than a baking oven. In the shade, it is ice cold.

Astronauts must wear special gravity suits to help them get around on the moon.

This astronaut became lost while collecting moon rocks. Help her get back to her spaceship.

Start

Finish

Great Craters!

The moon is covered with huge, round holes. These holes are called *craters*. Some of the moon's craters are so big that if you were to drive from one end of the crater to the other, it would take you an entire day!

Connect the dots from 1 to 25 for a surprise!

Star Light, Star Bright!

There are *billions and billions* of stars in the sky! On a clear night, you can probably see about 3,000 of them. Astronomers can see more stars when they look through a special instrument.

To find out the name of this special instrument, cross out the letters Z, Q, X, and Y. Write the leftover letters on the lines below.

Q T Z E X

Y X L Y E

S C Q Q O

Y P Z E Q

_ _ _ _ _ _ _ _ _

A Star Is Born

Long ago, people thought that groups of stars made pictures in the sky. They gave each group of stars a name.

To find out the names of the two groups of stars below, rearrange the letters in each word to form a new word. The first letter of each new word will spell out the secret names.

A. 1. GAB   __ __ __
     2. SIT   __ __ __
     3. SAG   __ __ __
     4. MOOD   __ __ __ __
     5. CHIN   __ __ __ __
     6. APE   __ __ __
     7. TIP   __ __ __
     8. ARE   __ __ __
     9. DEAR   __ __ __ __

THE __ __ __ __ , __ __ __ __ __ __

B. 1. DOOR   _ _ _ _ _
    2. PORE   _ _ _ _ _
    3. KIN   _ _ _ _
    4. SOAR   _ _ _ _ _
    5. PAN   _ _ _

    _ _ _ _ _

Planet-mania!

On a clear night you'll see many objects "lit up" in the sky. The tiny, twinkling dots are stars. On some nights, a few of those dots may seem bigger than others. If they are shining with a steady light and not twinkling, chances are they are not stars — they are planets!

There are nine planets in our solar system: Mercury, Venus, Earth, Mars, Jupiter, Saturn, Uranus, Neptune, and Pluto.

Circle the smallest planet.
Put an X on the largest planet.
Which planet is probably the coldest planet?
Which planet is probably the hottest?

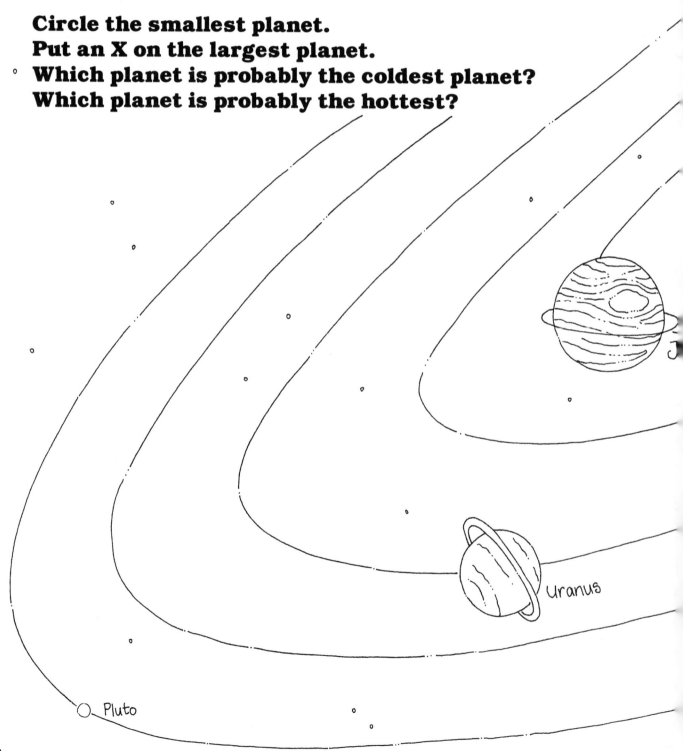

Uranus

Pluto

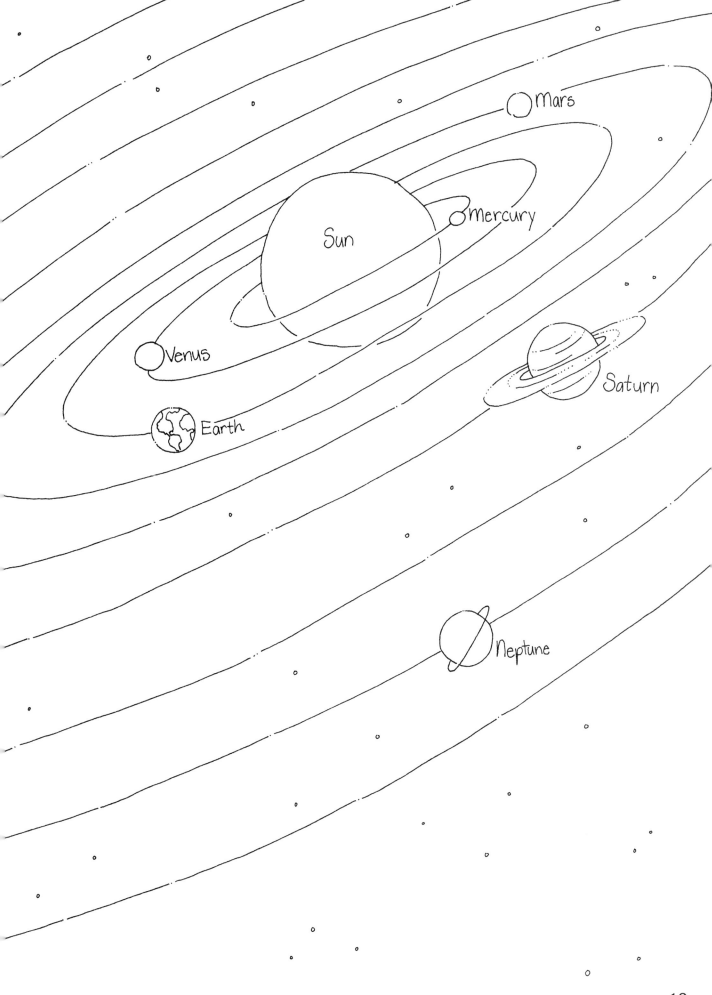

Planet Scramble

Each planet is unique. Unscramble the names of each one.

1. R E M U C R Y: The planet closest to the sun

   _ _ _ _ _ _ _

2. N E V U S: The brightest planet

   _ _ _ _ _

3. R A T E H: The only *known* planet with life

   _ _ _ _ _

4. S M R A: Called the "red planet" because of its reddish color

   _ _ _ _

5. T I P U J E R: The largest of all planets

   _ _ _ _ _ _ _

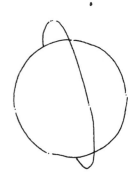

6. U S R A T N: Thousands of rings circle it

— — — — — —

7. N U S U A R: Scientists thought it was a star at first

— — — — — —

8. P U T N E E N: The "blue-green" planet

— — — — — — —

9. L U T O P: The coldest planet and the furthest from the sun

— — — — —

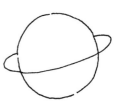

Hey, Where Did the Sun Go?

All nine planets circle the sun. The *moon* circles the earth. Sometimes the earth, the moon, and the sun become lined up in such a way that the moon actually blocks the sun from our view for a few minutes. Other times, the sun blocks the moon from our view. This is called an *eclipse*. A *solar eclipse* is when the moon is blocking the sun. A *lunar eclipse* is when the sun blocks the moon.

Some people like to watch a lunar eclipse through a telescope to see it up close.

Look at this scene very carefully. Then take the memory quiz on the next page.

How Good Is Your Memory?

Circle the picture in each scene that is exactly the same as the one on pages 22 and 23.

In a Flash!

Sometimes at night, a mysterious hazy patch of light moves slowly among the stars. As it travels it gets brighter and brighter, and then it fades and disappears! Scientists tell us that this strange "flash" is made up of glowing clumps of ice and dust. But is it a planet? A star? It isn't a planet *or* a star.

Use the code to spell out the name of this astronomical object.

M = ☆
C = ☾
T = ☄
E = ☀
O = ♄

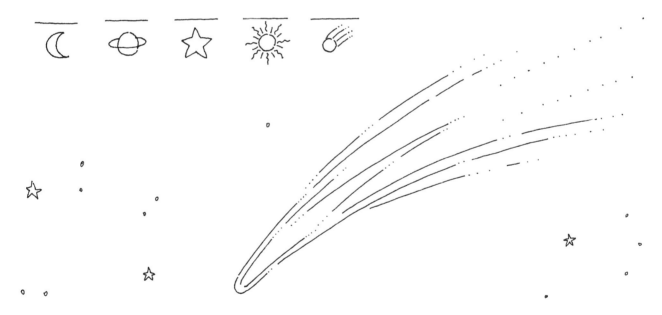

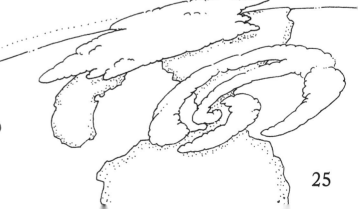

An Important Discovery!

An astronomer named Edmund Halley studied the paths of comets for years. He discovered a very unusual comet. This special comet traveled around the sun and *returned* about *every 76 years*! It was seen in 1834, 1910, and 1986.

The name of this famous comet is hidden in this roundabout puzzle. Begin at START and write every other letter in the puzzle boxes.

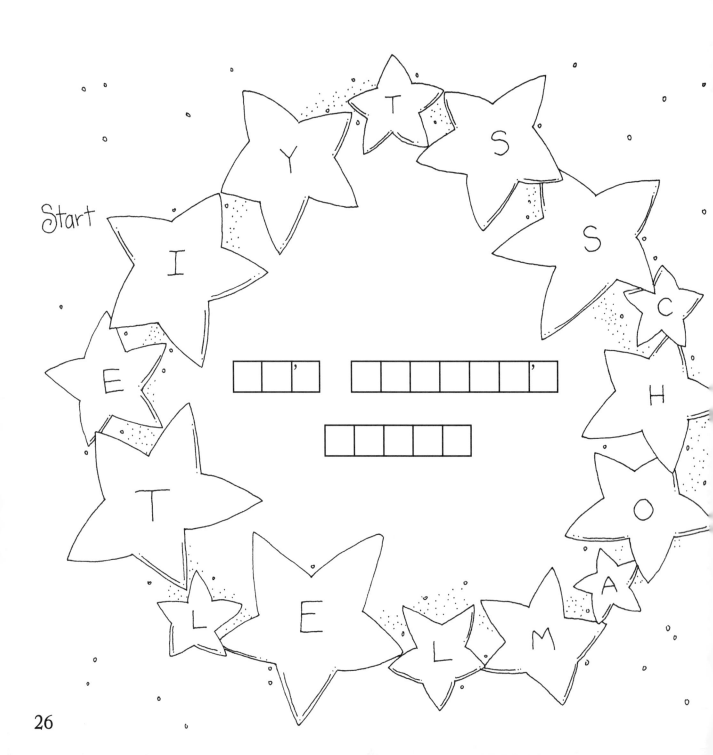

Was That a Shooting Star?

Shooting stars aren't really stars at all — they're *meteors*. Meteors are mostly small chunks of nickel and iron or broken bits of a comet that fly through the sky and burn up. The meteors that don't burn up, however, might make it through the earth's atmosphere and land on our planet! A meteor that hits the earth is called a *meteorite*.

Circle four things that do not belong in this picture.

27

Destination: Space!

Scientists send astronauts into space in order to learn more about our solar system. The astronauts travel in spaceships or space shuttles. People enjoy watching a space shuttle blast off from Earth. It is very exciting. They watch the shuttle climb higher and higher in the sky — until it disappears in space!

The launching scenes on these two pages are not alike. Circle the five things that are different.

U-do-it Universe!

Draw in the missing parts to this picture.

Puzzle Answers

Page 3. Sun-sational!

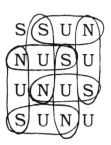

Page 4. What Is It?

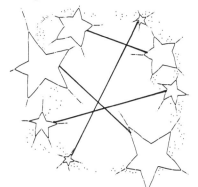

Page 5. Moon Struck!

Pages 8–9. Clouds, Clouds Everywhere!

Pages 10–11. Up and Away!

```
M O O N B D E B
N U S O A R A L
C B D S L M G R
A I R P L A N E
H R C L O U D S
I D S K O F O N
T S J H N E P Q
```

Pages 12–13. A-Mazing Moon Journey!

Page 14. Great Craters!

Page 15. Star Light, Star Bright!

TELESCOPE

Pages 16–17. A Star Is Born

A. 1. bag 2. its 3. gas 4. doom 5. inch 6. pea 7. pit 8. ear 9. read

THE BIG DIPPER

B. 1. odor 2. rope 3. ink 4. oars 5. nap

ORION

Pages 18–19. Planet-mania!
Pluto is probably the coldest planet.
Mercury is probably the hottest planet.

Page 20. Planet Scramble
1. MERCURY 2. VENUS 3. EARTH 4. MARS 5. JUPITER
6. SATURN 7. URANUS 8. NEPTUNE 9. PLUTO

Page 24. How Good Is
Your Memory?

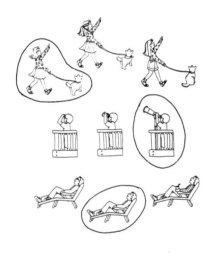

Page 25. In a
Flash!
COMET

Page 26. An
Important
Discovery!
IT'S
HALLEY'S
COMET

Page 27. Was That
a Shooting Star?

Pages 28–29. Destination:
Space!

Page 30. U-do-it Universe!